undress words

undress words
words undress

VOLUME ONE

P.S. From Delrose

QURAN DEES
CHANNIN DAVIS

KEEN VISION
PUBLISHING

Printed in the United States of America
Keen Vision Publishing, LLC
www.publishwithKVP.com
ISBN: 978-1-955316-43-9

*To our families and friends who always support us
throughout our journeys.*

*And...to everyone who showed us that love is valued
and the ones who used love for their value.*

Either way it was used.

contents

Dear You,

stumped	13
clutch	15
inside	16
familiar face	17
fairytales	18
SYL	19
the FLU	21
i tried	23
help	24
hats	26
the media	27
the edge	29
TKO	30
knock knock	31
those/them	33
homecoming side A	35
the art hur	37
smile	39
hypnotize	41
my love	43
sweet valentine	44

UNDRESS WORDS/WORDS UNDRESS

summer breeze   48
homecoming side B   50

P.S. From Delrose

over pain   53
untitled   54
glory runner   55
higher power   56
fein   57
snakes hiss   59
the present of meditation   60
untitled. . . .again   61
delrose's cry   63
mitri poetry   64
f.a.r.   66
controller   68
september   70
fwm²   71
love vs. lust   73
real love   75
her smile   77
roar   78
i hear your heart   79

stay connected   81

Delrose is clueless but is intrigued. He wants to open the gateway to his feelings and use that as a guide in a life he doesn't always understand.

Undressed Words/Words Undressed is a collection of poems and shorts stories written from the impact of Delrose's experiences...things that he could not express so he kept within.

dear you.

Stumped

Mother Nature put me in place
I'm handicapped and motionless
Cursed, huh?!

She took my voice away,
While leaving me to hear the annoying chirping of the
birds, also the snakes that hissssssssed through my grass...
Why couldn't she just take my sight, mother?

But am I alone?
I see one beautiful seed
growing next to my roots

Everyone embraced such beauty
And, yet, she clings to me
Such shade protects me from all this heat coming my way

Watching from up close
the storms come and go
while watering this delicate flower under me.

UNDRESS WORDS/WORDS UNDRESS

She's waiting for someone's arrival
Yet, I feel her sadness while hearing her cries
As no one appears but I've been here.

Less visits leave my leaves falling
Making me unnoticed by the shade that once protected
her.
She sees me no more.

From afar I see a garden full of snakes that whisper to me
Yet from her far she sees a tree now stumped from cuts for
not appearing to be who she thought I was

a tree...

clutch

While the faces count down the seconds
Everything moves in silence
Like the turtle & the hare I am racing for time.
I'm deaf to the crowd and all I hear is my thoughts
I feel the butterflies circling in my stomach
Time is not on my side as the eyes watch my every move!
Things are not appearing as they should while the basket
is bigger than ever
The time that plays in my head seems like forever
Will they respect me?
Do I have enough courage?
Time is ticking!!

5.. 4..3..2..1.

inside

So, I cracked the window
They smelled the aroma and wanted to taste my feelings.
I hear the doorbell.
 I wonder if I should open it or just leave it closed.
If I open it will they just wipe their feet off and leave every-thing behind?
Better yet, will they bring unnecessary baggage inside?
I should open it. I should lay out the red carpet.
 I did that last time and my most valuable things were stolen.
I never thought anyone would be outside again.
Maybe I should open my blinds so I can see the light from outside.
Nah.
I'll let it remain dark, so they will not see what goes on inside.
Sorry, love.
There's no way of getting inside again.

familiar face

I long for such a gentle touch from her heart.
Yet, in me
She sees similar traits from the one who betrayed her
heart
I approach her with a deep whisper to her soul,
I am not him.
Confused by what is being seen and heard
She is frightened.
She sees a familiar sight but it's blurry
Sounds much alike but different voices...
Physically, I'm who she wants to be with
She's just not mentally ready
cause all she can endure is that familiar face.

fairytales

I am not a knight with a shining armor.
I do not have an S on my chest.
I can't offer a glass slipper to my Cinder Ella,
Can't even wake my beauty up with a kiss.
I tried getting three wishes from the lamp
I asked Genie for love but Aladdin beat me to it.
My Bella never made it to the ball.
She was bitten and never seen or heard from again
Louis always had a thing for men with capes.
I tried to help Rapunzel let her hair down, but according to
her I pulled it out.
My apple didn't have poison, but Aurora still sent it back
by her dwarfs.
I loved little red, but she prefers wolves.
And the other girl left me for some porridge.
I guess I am a beast to all these beauties.
It just wasn't meant for me to find someone.
One day I'll have my own fairytale.

SYL

When do you know a bye is really a goodbye?
Who would have known when I dropped you off
that would be the last time
I was afraid to attend the funeral
Me being the one to blame and all
I was the last person to see you alive
 I said "bye" but meant to say "see you later."
I did not expect that bye to really be a goodbye,
Seems like just the other day you was throwing off the wall
in the hoop wit Kibrom,
hell who would have thought you and cheese bunny helped
fight them dudes at the pool
 we always called next on Wednesday and Saturday.
Crazy.
Bruh would never let us play with the old heads on Sunday
still midway's finest.
We always had our 5
 me (point guard)
 you (shooting guard)
 Chris (power forward)

Rico (center)
Eric (small forward/shooting guard)
And of course
Our coack K
Kibrom joking on everyone who came to play us.
I pass
You shoot.
still undefeated
just one loss: You
But we still got next
I never made it to your funeral because I did not know how
to say good-bye
Yet your momma always mentioned never to say goodbye
So see you later, my brother.
love you, boy
Luther Bryant #11
Midway forever

the FLU

another trembling and sweaty night
a fiend for the love we once shared
i see myself interacting in our past arguments as we make
up
not realizing
i am by myself apologizing and no one is on my phone.
rocking back and forth
asking myself, "where did we go wrong?"
wishing yoU were here to wash away my endless tears for
yoU
saying, "baby, i'm sorry. hold me."
the only thing i am holding is a pillow
shivering as the night grows colder
you're not here to warm me up
i'm going crazy
every time i write
i am writing your name
i'm tripping.
trying to rehabilitate from our love and the years we were
together

but there is no remedy
it's not working
i am tossing and turning as i sleep
dreaming of us back together
i can't stop thinking about yoU
i can't get yoU out of my system
there are no antibiotics that can heal my heart
i can't leave cause everywhere i go, i see yoU
i can't hear the phone without thinking it's yoU
i'm a junky for a love I can't have
i've lost my mind,
yoU were the best thing I had in life
now this cold has become the FLU
because i'm Forever Loving yoU.

Tried

I tried to become the man of your dreams not the one you fear

I try to cook yet you say the taste is so bitter

I tried to be positive, but you throw the negatives at me

I tried to make you smile but you still frown from his mistakes

I tried opening my hands, yet you close yours

I tried listening yet you don't talk

I tried blessing you with my heart

but you won't open yours

I put my past away yet I saw you as my future

I tried talking yet you still ignore me

I tried to tell you I'm not them nor him

but you still saw me as one those

I tried to gain your trust, but the truth is

I'm tired of trying...

help

I wonder can they hear me since I have been screaming
this for a while.
Let me text them!! (left on read)
Double text..
Okay.
Let me call them for the millionth time
Hey... once you receive this message... give me a call.

Wait
Let me write it down
I do not think people close to me see it or me

Let me put it in a song with a gun or knife to my head
better yet
a rope
Maybe they will get the visual
What if I put it on a shirt?
Then, I can rest.
Hey, it may be the top seller.
Excuse me, friend

Hello?!
Can you hear me
can you see me
do you understand the words that are coming out of my
mouth?
Okay.
Wait.
I know how to get their attention.
let me tweet it (no retweets),
umm snapchat? (not one view)
IG? (no likes)
No, wait!
Tic tok!
They will finally watch me do it (not me)
Hell, it may be the trending topic with the most views?
Well, I am gone now
Crazy.
They still won't find me
even when I shared my location.
I wonder if they ever noticed.
Probably not
because all I was said whenever they asked
is, "I'm okay."

hats

They say I am a man of many hats
the one hat I haven't put on yet is "father."
I'm not running away from my responsibilities
nor have I given up.
Just afraid that it won't fit for many reasons,
I tried it on but it got bent out of shape
Too many hands trying to shape it.
I lost that hat to someone else she is more familiar with.
I'm a man with many hats
Just not the one I would like to wear every day.

the media

I used to hear the old folks talk about it
Yet it's past their time
Do they even do that anymore?
Nervous at this point
The thought of dm'ing you
Was just a thought
knowing that if she knew who I was
she would block me
So, I chose the old fashioned way
I wrote it.
She'll probably think I am a stalker
I can only admire her beauty from a distance
I get nervous just being around her
So I learn her from a far
Probably won't know I even exist.
scared she won't take it
I can't even say hey without stuttering
and losing all my train of thought
Who am I to write this?
She may not feel as I do.

Wait.
I'm not in love with her
just seeing if I can get her to fall for me in numerous of
ways while being around her.
What if she's not who I expected her to be?
I'm still willing to see.
The cost of humiliation on social media
Hmm...
I just pray she think this sweet
take of picture and cherish the moment..
who knows..
So, I wrote it?
I like you.
Do you like me?
Circle yes
maybe
or hell no

the edge

I've been to this breaking part of my life
where I'm at the edge but not quite ready to jump
I hear my people encouraging me to jump
yet I see the strangers who hope I won't
I'm on the edge but I'm ready to risk it all
Yet I stumble to the one I called love
A familiar face.
As I look up
our hands are slipping
She looks back to her past and lets go of her future.

It's not even the 1st round and they're already betting
against me
Being patient got me impatient
I guess that's God way of telling me to stop looking
Wait until it hits me in the face
like a TKO
I am still in the 1st round
willing to go 12
Damn.
I'm down for the count
10... 9... 8... 7...

knock knock

Knock, Knock
Who's there?
Me!
Me who?
Que!
Que who?
You told me
To knock for the opportunity
Funny how the voice changed
Sorry.
wrong door.
What about this door?
Knock, Knock
Come in. Who are you?
You know me!
I do not!
You told me if I ever needed help or support
Your door would always be open.
Sorry.
Wrong door.

Door closes.

This next one has to be the right one.

Knock, Knock

Who is it?

Me!

Me who?

Que!

Que who?

Sorry, I don't have time today.

Try again never!

Then, a door opens.

Come in, Que.

I heard you been knocking around.

You never knocked at this door

You don't know me.

But come in.

Wipe your feet on the welcome mat

and bring yourself to the table.

Your seat has been waiting.

those/them

I was chosen out of the few
yet they label me one of those
You heard the rumors
And wonder if they are true.
Could I be them or one of those?
who overlooked your heart?
Or one of them who cherished it
while listening to the beat
Yet again
the whisper still gives you chills
Those who see me, see me.
Not them or those.
For those outside looking in
Really trying to get inside to be one of them.
Honestly, it was just a friendly hey or goodbye
That led to a rumor
that labeled me one of those
I would rather be one of them that you connect with in
every aspect
There's no future in the past

UNDRESS WORDS/WORDS UNDRESS

See me as me
Instead of labeling me as one of those.

homecoming Side A

It is crazy how we stumble across things we've been
searching for our whole lives.
Why today?
Washing while packing up for a business trip, I come
across some lingerie that appeared out of nowhere. I know
I not tripping.
I start reminiscing.
OMG.
I was under a Love spell from her smell.
I knew she was coming from a mile away
I enter the closet and grab a shoe box
another one falls
The box
That held all her pictures
and the ring pop she gave me.
Am I tweaking?
Or is God telling me something?
Crazy.
I am in the closet reminiscing on such a southern belle
If this picture could talk.

hell, if college dorms' walls could talk
man...
Looking back I can hear her whispering my name
as I look back
I had to lay back on the floor and close my eyes
as if she were here
lying on my chest
endless nights as we spent laughing at me
instead of my lame jokes
her smile, her laughter, & her eyes made me do strange
things
she would stare at me
I would go in for a kiss
Suddenly my phone rings
And my thoughts leave
I throw the picture and kick the box over
Running to the phone.
It is the crew
hyped about Homecoming
I'm excited, but still in thought.
About her
Looking at the ring pop
Wonder if she has a man and kids now
Am I excited about Homecoming?
Or just the possibility of seeing her?

theart hin

A queen's first born to a king's second seed
I was born where the apples fell not too far from the falling
towers
A place where sweet Georgia peaches are raised in the hot
sun.
A seed that grew into a six foot canvas
My art becomes a display of my life.
Each tattoo, scar, and heartbreak tell a story of a battle I
faced
or a time death seemed near
My facial expression contradicts the genuine emotions I
hold inside
just like a seed
I was planted
but no one wanted me to grow

Life has been a road of unexpected events and downfalls
I use the doubt as motivation to push forward
Most believe, as a man, our hands are made to build
Yet, I use mine to create tales to feed the next generation's

imagination
a different outlook on story telling.
 I can never find the words to talk,
only the words to write a story
that explains my silence.

Smile

They say love is a beautiful thing
once u experience it...
the most unique feature I ever experienced was her smile.
Which I miss the most
 it warms my spirit at the coldest times of my life.
With such innocence
 It's like magic
yet it teases me
 she bites down on her bottom lip
with one eyebrow lifted up
she has something up her sleeve.
I could tell what she was thinking
Her smile always dictated her next move
she never frowns
I made sure of that
in every way she wants
she is pleased.
her smile makes my skin crawl
as if her lips are going up and down my body
even when she falls asleep in my arms

she's smiling.
Her smile means so much to me
it touches my soul like no other
even through a crowd
I can find her
by her smile...
I guess am blinded by it
It's the only thing I see
that shines on my heart.

hypnotize

Look into my eyes
No.
Don't turn your head.
Look as my brown hazel eyes hypnotize you
I see you
biting your lips.
I hear you
Your heart is racing
Come closer
And let these gentle arms wrap around you
I want to control your every move.
Listen as I whisper summer breeze through your ear.
Close your eyes as I blow night winds through your body.
Now relax as I lay you back on this soft cloud.
I feel your soul burning for desire.
Tune your ears to the rain as it gets you wet.
Open your eyes.
Can you see the smoke from my soul for you?
We should embrace such a moment.
Don't you agree?

UNDRESS WORDS/WORDS UNDRESS

The moment our bodies have been yearning for
Slowly
As the night awakens
So does my beauty
She asks, "What happened last night?"
I said, "You were hypnotized by the night's beauty."

my love

I remember the day I put eyes on you
Even remember when I sneaked out just to come see you
Car, bus, plane
Hell, even a horse
I'll walk miles just to be in your presence
You are My stress reliever
 my escape from this crazy world
You make me smile like no other
They got nothing on you
I hate the one person that we have between us
Our alone time together is very well spent
We don't agree on alot things
especially our early mornings
Yet I wake up excited just to feel you
The day they take you from me is the day I lose love for the game of basketball

Sweet Valentine

She sits and wonders what the night may be like
She hasn't seen me all day.
She paces back and forth
Cause she hasn't heard from me on the day of love.
I call at the top of the hour
9:00pm
Shhh....
Don't be mad.
Just listen.
Don't say a word.
Unlock the door and go under your pillow
See that blind fold?
Put it on.
She laughs and says okay.
I walk in and guide her toward our destination
"What you got up your sleeves?" she asks.
"Be patient," I reply. "We're almost there."
We enter our room
It's loud with the aroma of her favorite flames of passion
She's all smiles.

"Can I take this off?" she asks as she tugs at the blindfold.
"Hell naw," I reply. "But I'm about to take off your clothes."
She laughs as I gently undress her.
She trembles. She's nervous.
But I assure her there's no need.
I wrap a towel around her and lead her to a warm bubble
bath with candles.
She sits in and relaxes in water and rose petals.
I tell her I'll have dessert first
breakfast last.
As she lays in the tub I feed her chocolate covered straw-
berries and grapes.
She breathes heavily as the tip of my fingers touch her slip-
pery body
She bites her lips as I go deeper insider her with my hands.
She grabs my hand and tells me to stop
I laugh...
"Can I take this off? Again, she asks.
I whisper in her ear, "Just give me five more minutes."
I leave her alone to get dressed and tell her she can remove
the blindfold.
"Follow the trail of Hershey kisses," I say as I close the
door.
She follows the trail to the master bedroom
A field of roses and a 7 foot teddy bear beside
the fireplace with
a Kays jewelry box.
as she opens the box, she sees inside a ring pop and a letter
Do you wove me?
Circle yes, no, or maybe

She laughs at the letter and the ring pop
I sneak up from behind and kiss her neck
Her eyes get low.
I kiss and lick her lower back
Then slowly laid her on the bed...
I feel her heartbeat as I nibble on her breasts
With ice between my lips
Stroking her body up and down as it melts
I soak it up with my tongue as she quivers
My lips slowly kiss her inner thighs and my fingertips
follow
She grabs the sheets.
I taste her wet passionate insides between my lips with my
new tongue tricks
She gasps in sweet surrender as she reaches out to stop me

Her hunger for passion is in my control
Our bodies bond as one
From the floor
to the fireplace
back to the bed.
In the shower
out the shower
Hot, passionate sex in every position she can think of.
I grip the arch in her back as she rides me
Screaming for more.
Her nails dig into my back
She yells "I'm coming."
Every time I hit her g spot.
As the moon sleeps

and the sun awakes

I approached my sweet valentine with eggs

Grits, toast, and sausage.

A glass of OJ that I squeezed with my own hands.

"I have never been touched, licked, kissed, nibbled, and sucked liked that before."

She doesn't have to tell me.

I already know.

All of that last night for Valentine's? She asks.

"Naw, I don't need a special day to show you how I feel."

I reply.

"To be honest, this breakfast is your Valentine's Day present."

LOL

Summerbreeze

The night leaks out of the evening sky
Stars peek at me and twinkle through your hazel eyes.
As you gaze upon the moonlight
It shines on your carmel complexion.
Another lonely night.
I gently sneak through the cracks of your room
So you can feel my every move
While you relax and settle in, I'll just whisper a breeze that
sends chills down your spine
No need to look back as if someone was there
You can't see me
You can only feel me.
As you lie in bed
I'll continue whispering things
that make your body quiver.
A gentle blow toward your body
that makes your soul burn for more.
My breeze is like the tip of an ice cube
Rubbing down your body slowly
As your eyes rolls and your toes curls!

UNDRESS WORDS/WORDS UNDRESS

Stop grabbing the sheets and feel my breeze
Let it fulfill your every desire
Before you fall fast asleep.
I sneak back out the window just as the sun rises
She waits patiently for another midnight summer breeze.

homecoming Side B

They say old things bring good memories.
I ran across an old shirt I use to sleep in.
I figured I threw it away
Crazy how I stumble on things.
Since all this pandemic stuff is finally over
The world is getting back to normal.
And my mind is filled with memories about days in Normal.
I ain't normal
Not after finding this.
I can still smell his scent on this shirt.
A quick flash back in the mirror of his sweet whispers
The pulling,
The kissing,
The smacking
And his warmth gentle touch around my neck.
 Oh My Gawd
His sex language is an unknown tongue
But it always got my juices flowing.

Now I'm grabbing my neck and trying to slide my hand
down my...
Wait...
What has come over me?
I instantly throw the shirt across the room as if it were
cursed.
Then a text comes through
Messy at its finest.
A group message from the crew saying, "Homecoming
about to be too lit! The Rona gone!"
I don't know how to reply to the girls.
All they are talking about is seeing their old boos, sneaky
links, and girl crushes.
All I can think of is him.
It's just a shirt.
Hell.
 I think it was his scent
Or maybe I am dicknotized by a southern gentleman I have
been yearning for years.
See that's my problem
That's why I blocked him.
I know he has questions.
Maybe he doesn't.
Maybe he's in a relationship.
Maybe he's got a dope marriage with kids, big house, white
picket fence.
A family dog.
Things I used to wish we had.
I probably shouldn't tell the girls.
They might amp me up to text him.

I don't think I'm ready
Or, maybe...
I am?

P.S. From Delrose

over pain

Pain is just words unsaid
Words unsaid equals pain in your head.
Headaches from over-thinking develops thoughts that should be said.
Why must I suffer from the pain in my head?
Why can't I run away and my thoughts stay in place?
Truth of the matter is
Thoughts are placed but you can run all day.
Think about it.
Over the pain is just a way of getting out of the race.
The race that you can pace.
Your race is your race.
So, pain is over when you run at your pace.

untitled

Realize that people are people
Take your time to find your peace.
Before opening your heart for others
Close the truth within yourself.
Don't fall in love with the idea of me.
Don't dive into my mind until you are ready to be pleased
by a sapiosexual.
Losing yourself inside of me can cost you your truth.

glory runner

Chase the things you love
Stand for the one you love
To get the glory you have to have a story.

higher power

I will go through hell and high waters to understand the
fire in your ocean.
That's a pun that turns into a pond.
I'd rather intersect with your intellect that leads not to sex.
I want that deep love from within that doesn't take moon-
shine and gin
Flowing like your hair just like the rivers inside is what I
dream of.
Now baby tell me
What are you dreaming of?

Fein

To the woman of my dreams
I apologize.
Nightmares are here.
But they tell no lie.
I cause some to Fein.
For the thing I have waiting for you on the inside.
I call 'em crazy.
Really
They just caring.
Delusional
They just dedicated.
Really?
I'm just irritated.
With the fact, connecting with them is like sprint.
Bright enough to grab my attention.
But this shit is about to end quick.
I study my roles
Played all of the tapes
But I still can't figure out what sense does it make.
To take the only thing I have left to put through the test.

UNDRESS WORDS/WORDS UNDRESS

Yet I stay stressed.

Feeling the holiest matrimony when I'm around you

But feelings urge to mess with her too.

But only I can assure you.

I know my dream is to be with you.

Yes

I had nightmares

I can't lie.

But to the woman of my dreams,

I do

'Til the day I die.

Snakes kiss

I want to let my snake sneak inside your walls.
As you inhale all of your deep applause.
Cascading down my snake in your mind
You're praying: please don't leave.
I hiss into your ear deadly things
But in your mind
You're getting deceived.
Life and death are in the power of the tongue.
You're that wet
And I haven't even unbuckled my pants yet.

the present of meditation

Looking beyond the mind of an average man.
I live with humbleness creating this being that belongs to
creation.
I will only succeed with the support of myself.
Deeper my mind dives in the waters of the world
Places my outer man can only dream.
I open my mind with this water that seems to slow down
time then.
You come around.
You have this present that I can't wrap but only present.

untitled...again

Everything isn't how it's supposed to be.
I never did anything else besides be myself, you see.
My heart is too big for me to miss the small things.
Why me?
That's all I ask for wisdom and guidance.
My pain is worth nothing for others
But my love is giving with all hustle.
I hurt myself trying to learn with no vision
I want to be good but with no precision.
According to the associated
Im just accepted
A wanna be.
I don't want anyone that has to be in glory for light.
I want to be myself just for the rest of my life.
Open to private things and no diamond.
I was hurt that I was here being the honest.
Yes.
I had my faults
But I didn't mind telling you that I wasn't good.
It's so much I want to tell you

but not yet.
I'm still misunderstood.
With one strike from this pen
I can spill all of my secrets within.
The mishaps of the past will forever linger within.
The pain that I hide to keep the smile inside.

delyse's cry

The fear of being alone scares us the most
To the point we forget that fear is a mindset.
It's a setup for us to believe that with you,
I'm going to be hurt
And without you,
I'm going to be lonely.
I really wish that they could clone me
So I can see the scary things from my point of view
And yours too.
It seems like I can never please
but only deceive
Or, maybe it's me.
My mindset is set on getting mine.
Instead of understanding minds.
Praying is the right answer
But I'm so wrong.
Mindset is not even my own
It's set on others' minds instead of mine.
So far gone.

mtri poetry

Looking beyond the mind of an average man.
I live with humbleness creating this being that belongs to creation.
I will only succeed with the support of myself.
Deeper my mind dives in the waters of the world
Places my outer man can only dream.
I open my mind with this water that seems to slow down time then.
You come around.
You have this present that I can't wrap but only present.

UNDRESS WORDS/WORDS UNDRESS

Poetry is a way to communicate feelings in sceneries.
Your love is above and beyond the birds and clouds itself.
The galaxy with millions of different stars with bright
lights and shine so far.

f.a.r.

The far has a deeper meaning than the average human can
see.
But you seem to understand that like no else.
Fear. Appreciation. Reaction.
See, you saw my start when I was too young to understand
it.
You didn't let fear sink in because you took time to dive in
to the deep
And stop FEAR FROM GETTING TO ME.
And when I did wrong
You put fear in my heart all because you loved me.
You led me to the start line
And when I began to run
You supported me
APPRECIATED ME.
CORRECTED ME.
BUT SUPPORTED ME.
AND ALL BECAUSE YOU LOVED ME.
WHEN I GET DEEP IN THE RACE
I LOOK FOR YOU AND THERE YOU ARE.

UNDRESS WORDS/WORDS UNDRESS

Your REACTION gives me strength.

Even when I'm in my wrong.

Your reaction gives me strength to become a better man.

I'm glad that I have a Mother who will go the distance and stretch the strength.

Thank you Mom for going F. A. R.

controller

Control what you can control because
once you try to control something you CAN'T control
you lose control
over the things you CAN.
Ships Carrying Relations
There are times when your name will be tossed back and
forth
Leaving you in awe or shocked.
You are no longer a human with rights.
Just a human that everyone knows from the night.
You speak up and you're called egotistical.
But I say I didn't call my ego to be a sense of enjoyment.
I've proven myself to be strong.
But strength can become weakness in a time of need.
I say that to say.
I'm cutting the ends that hung on to drag me down.
My dream is bigger than my reality
But really my itch for being rich can cause a sink to a ship
that contains relations.
I'm proud of who I am and what I see

UNDRESS WORDS/WORDS UNDRESS

I'm glad that the toughest path choose me.
Now I pray for each of my foes and my prey.
This long ship that sinks with relations is as warm as a
mink.
I will provide for my foes and my prey.
Because at the end of the day
I'M victorious
because I paved a greater way.

September

Well if I was to tell a story of a book would you look?

Can I intrigue your mind just by the look?

Can I capture your imagination with just one pure touch?

Are you will to open up this book?

If you do decide to fall for this hardback book

Let's see how deep your mind is to feel this look.

My pure touch captivates all of you to my chamber of pages.

Will have you wanting to move lumber in the month September.

Do not get lost when you fall like lumber in the month of September

You have me in your purest form of captivity.

Mentally you're all mine already.

When will you ever admit it?

FWM²

Fine Wine Melanin Mastermind

You are so fine.
Your eyes couldn't compare to the vision of the master
mind.
Masterpiece in the form of a melanin coat.
Dripping of things I could provoke.
If only she would let me get close to see the fine wine mela-
nin mastermind.
Only in due time.
Could I count this dime?
Spend a lifeline?
Just to make me feel like my life is worth more than a lime.
But only if I could sip this fine glass of wine.
With this melanin coat color.
That takes over like a mastermind.
Put together like a masterpiece in my mind.
My vision becomes blurry as I walk along this line.
It's not just your average penny drink
It's along the dime line.
It's topped off with this lime.
This drink is passion beyond the regulars.

UNDRESS WORDS/WORDS UNDRESS

This fine wine melanin mastermind master piece could
make you spend your last dime
Makes it hard to walk down the line.
It can change your life.
With just a sip of this fine wine.

love vs. lust

Is beauty a given?
Or, is it taken?
Between my lens you're the perfect craft.
A goddess's smile is what you have.
Yet again, I ask.
Is beauty given or taken?
Perhaps you are the shine to my inner circle.
The Sun is what people began to see
But they never notice until the sun ceases.
Yet again, I ask.
Is the beauty given or taken?
Love is a decision.
I never knew the difference.
Lust is the inner man striking with his vision.
Yet again, I ask.
Is beauty given or taken?
Beauty is both.
But what is our vision?
Do we see eye to eye to eye?
3 eyes?

UNDRESS WORDS/WORDS UNDRESS

I must apologize for my dearest mistake
I meant Me, Myself, and I.
Selfishness is great a deserted island filled with loneliness
and silence.
The irony of us making it to where we are, baby
It's both of our faults.
Beauty is both.
What if You leave me for my past you see?
I'll be discredited and disoriented to the point
I search in the opposite sex.
Same parts like you.
With the warmest heart.
I open them to same story
These females won't see the credits at the end.
Their souls will feel in debt to me because I see nothing
more than one thing.
See your glasses and my vision of happiness and passion.
Passing the opening Ceremony of the Happiest girl.
Even Joy And Hope would even become addicted to dope.
So Beauty is both.
If you live it's given
But if you leave it's taken.
My question now is
Who is really in control?

real love

It hurts me when you constantly say how I don't notice
stuff that you do.
Look at the shoe on the other foot.
I constantly involve you in everything that I do
And I don't mind letting people know that I care for you
Because that's what a gentleman does.
But I just get tired
Everything I do is good and sweet
When it benefits you.
But when it doesn't
It's something I'm lacking
And how do you think that makes me feel?
Why should you be sweet, considering, concerned, and
acute.
I never ask for much.
But we both stated somethings that should keep this going
But ...
Baby girl, why do you hustle so hard for yourself
And trip on the one that's behind you?
Pushing you.

UNDRESS WORDS/WORDS UNDRESS

Holding you when you are scared.
Will take the stabs in the back for you.
Doesn't mind giving 200% in this relationship.
Because once that person feels enough pain
And they decide to let go
You are going to start feeling all that pain at once.
But you're going to be so hurt
Because you felt like the person who was behind you was
useless
Until you mature and realize how much he cared.
Because someone who truly know what love is
WILL NEVER EVER tell you or BOAST about what they are
doing right
But this is how you know that they really love you.
Because when he is on the ground dying
And is in pain
Not because of the pain that he took for your sake.
He is really hurting
Because he can't tell you everything he has done for you
Because he doesn't want you to feel any worse than you
already do.
He cares for you SO MUCH
And LOVES YOU SO MUCH
That he is willing to hide his back from you
So you don't see the pain that he has taken for you.

her Smile

See I was timid to let you get close to
This thing that pumps my chest
The smile you give can change my mood
From sun to moon
To sun back to you.
It's bigger than you think shit to be quite frankly.
That alone can start my day.
I know it's only a quarter of a day but
Now I see why my mommy says save.
Because if I get that same smile all day
Every day
I'm a rich man in the heart and the soul.
Girl, you forever make me feel bold.
You are beyond the meek
And you work harder than a man working at a paper mill.
But what truly miss I can't say.
Unless you say YES.
Then, baby
I will reveal all of me that remains.

roar

The heart of a lion is fearless
Less for the pack brings more for the hunt.
The lioness is the protector of her own
But her pride produces a problem
Pay attention to the heart of lion
Because her pride will bring less for the nest.

i hear your heart

There is no greater feeling
Than being with you
Being in your presence
It's similar to mental healing
You take me to a happy place
Where I feel the summer breeze
Like I'm walking Down a road
And each side is crowded with towering trees
You make me feel beautiful
and delicate
Like a lotus flower
I love the sound of your voice,
But you heart speaks louder.

Stay connected

Thank you for reading *Undress Words/Words Undress Volume One: P.S. From Delrose.* Here are a few ways you can connect with the authors.

FACEBOOK	Channin Davis
	Quran Dees
INSTAGRAM	@mogulimagesllc
	@lightweightque
WEBSITE	www.thedemocollection.com

www.ingramcontent.com/pod-product-compliance
Lightning Source LLC
Chambersburg PA
CBHW070829250626
47170CB00006B/2259